Sink and Float

Written by Margaret MacDonald

Picture Dictionary

glass things

metal things

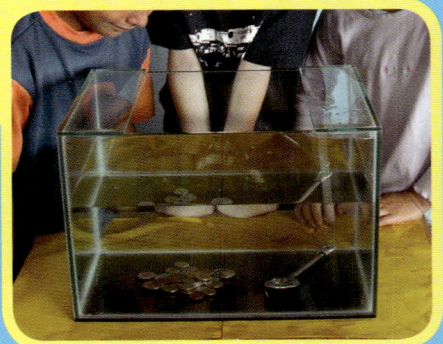

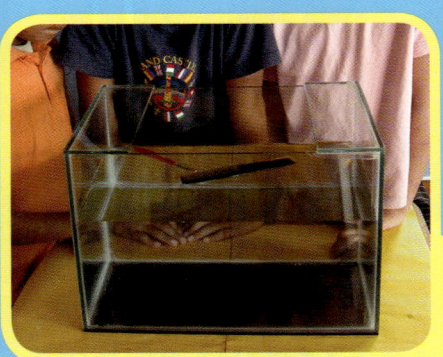

plastic things

Read the picture dictionary. You will find these words in the book.

rubber balls

tank

wooden things

Look at these things.
Some are heavy.
Some are light.
Some have air inside them.
Some will float
and some will sink.

We tested things
by putting them
in a tank of water.
Look at the plastic things
in the water.
They are floating.

Can you see
the metal things
in the water?
The metal things
are at the bottom
of the tank.
Metal things are heavy,
so they sink.

Look at the rubber balls
in the water.
The rubber balls
are floating.
They have air inside them,
which makes them float.

Can you see
the glass things in the tank?
The glass things have sunk.
They are heavy,
so they have sunk
to the bottom of the tank.

Are the wooden things floating or sinking? The wooden things are floating in the water. Wooden things are light, so they can float.

Activity Page

Find out for yourself what sinks and what floats. Put these things in a bowl of water.

    coin   pencil
    comb   stone
    key   tennis ball
    marble toothbrush

Write which things floated and which sank. Group the things together.

Do you know the dictionary words?